Kylie Jean

Valentine Queen

by Marci Peschke

illustrated by Tuesday Mourning

PICTURE WINDOW BOOKS
a capstone imprint

Kylie Jean is published by Picture Window Books
A Capstone Imprint
1710 Roe Crest Drive
North Mankato, Minnesota 56003
www.capstonepub.com

Library of Congress Cataloging-in-Publication Data
Peschke, M. (Marci), author.
    Valentine queen / by Marci Peschke ; illustrated by Tuesday Mourning.
        pages cm. -- (Kylie Jean)
    ISBN 978-1-4795-2352-8 (hardcover) -- ISBN 978-1-4795-3814-0 (paper over board)
1. Valentine's Day--Texas--Juvenile fiction. 2. Wedding anniversaries--Texas--Juvenile fiction. 3.
Families--Texas--Juvenile fiction. 4. Parties--Texas--Juvenile fiction. 5. Elementary schools--Texas-
-Juvenile fiction. 6. Texas--Juvenile fiction. [1. Valentine's Day--Fiction. 2. Old age--Fiction. 3. Family
life--Fiction. 4. Parties--Fiction. 5. Schools--Fiction. 6. Texas--Fiction.] I. Mourning, Tuesday, illustrator.
II. Title. III. Series: Peschke, M. (Marci) Kylie Jean.
    PZ7.P441245Val 2014
    813.6--dc23
                                        2013028545

Summary: Kylie Jean's grandparents fiftieth wedding anniversary is on Valentine's Day, and the whole
family is planning a surprise party--but Kylie also wants her class to spread valentine cheer to Oak
Manor, the local assisted living facility.

Graphic Designer: Kristi Carlson
Editor: Alison Deering
Production Specialist: Eric Manske

Design Element Credit:
Shutterstock/blue67design

Printed in China.
092013
007738LEOS14

For the REAL true Nanny,
with love for Rick
—MP

Table of Contents

All About Me, Kylie Jean!

My name is Kylie Jean Carter. I live in a big, sunny, yellow house on Peachtree Lane in Jacksonville, Texas, with Momma, Daddy, and my two brothers, T.J. and Ugly Brother.

T.J. is my older brother, and Ugly Brother is . . . well . . . he's really a dog. Don't you go telling him he is a dog. Okay? I mean it. He thinks he is a real, true person.

He is a black-and-white bulldog. His front looks like his back, all smashed in. His face is all droopy like he's sad, but he's not.

His two front teeth stick out, and his tongue hangs down. (Now you know why his name is Ugly Brother.)

Everyone I love to the moon and back lives in Jacksonville. Nanny, Pa, Granny, Pappy, my aunts, my uncles, and my cousins all live here. I'm extra lucky, because I can see all of them any time I want to!

My momma says I'm pretty. She says I have eyes as blue as the summer sky and a smile as sweet as an angel. (Momma says pretty is as pretty does. That means being nice to the old folks, taking care of little animals, and respecting my momma and daddy.)

But I'm pretty on the outside and on the inside. My hair is long, brown, and curly.

I wear it in a ponytail sometimes, but my absolute most favorite is when Momma pulls it back in a princess style on special days.

I just gave you a little hint about my big dream. Ever since I was a bitty baby I have wanted to be an honest-to-goodness beauty queen. I even know the wave. It's side to side, nice and slow, with a dazzling smile. I practice all the time, because everybody knows beauty queens need to have a perfect wave.

I'm Kylie Jean, and I'm going to be a beauty queen. Just you wait and see!

Chapter 1
Sweethearts

Can you keep a secret? Because I have a big one to tell you. Here it goes . . . our whole family is planning a surprise anniversary party for Nanny and Pa! Everyone knows they were real, true high school sweethearts. They will have been married for fifty years this Valentine's Day.

All of the grown-ups in my family are sitting around our dining room table talking about party ideas. My best cousin, Lucy, and I are sitting quietly on the floor with Ugly Brother and listening.

"Nanny and Pa have been in love for a long, long time," Lucy whispers. "They deserve a party! I sure hope it's as nice as they are."

I nod in agreement. "I wish Nanny were here to tell us their story," I say. "But then the party wouldn't be a surprise."

Then an idea hits my brain like red stripes on a peppermint stick! "Let's tell each other a story!" I suggest. "I'll start. When Nanny and Pa were in high school, Pa was a football star, just like T.J."

Lucy picks up the story. "Nanny was the new girl in town, and she didn't know anyone, boys or girls. That made her feel nervous on her first day at Jacksonville High School."

"Don't forget it was because she was shy, too!" I chime in.

Lucy nods. "That's right!" she says. "Then Nanny got mixed up and went to the wrong classroom. Pa was in his science class when Nanny walked in wearing a pink poodle skirt. She looked as pretty as a picture. It was love at first sight for Pa. When the teacher realized Nanny was in the wrong place —"

"Pa offered to walk Nanny to her English class," I finish. "Nanny didn't say a word, but Pa talked the whole way because then he was nervous. And when they got to the right classroom, Nanny looked into Pa's big brown eyes, and she fell in love, too."

Suddenly it's so quiet I could hear a spider spin a web. Lucy and I look up and realize that the whole family is listening to us tell Nanny and Pa's love story.

Momma smiles at us. "They loved each other so much they decided to get married on Valentine's Day."

Suddenly all of the grown-ups start talking at once. You might not know it, but planning a big party is a lot of work! Nobody seems to have an idea that everyone can agree on, and Lucy and I are getting bored.

"Let's play a game!" I tell Lucy. "When someone says 'love,' we'll eat a candy heart."

Ugly Brother barks excitedly, "Ruff, ruff!" That means yes. He wants to play, too, but I think he really just wants to eat candy.

"Okay, you can play, too," I tell him, "but you'd better be listening, or you're not getting any candy."

Ugly Brother sits at attention. He doesn't have to wait too long before someone mentions putting lovebirds on the cake.

"I love that idea!" our cousin Lilly says.

Lucy and I grin at each other. It's a good thing we have a bowl full of heart candies! Lucy and I each get two. Ugly Brother whines, so we give him two candies, too.

"How about red roses and daisies as the centerpieces for the tables?" Aunt Suzie suggests. "Those are the flowers Nanny had at her wedding, so they'd be just perfect for her party."

Lucy and I glance at each other. That idea doesn't get us any candy. While we wait, we look through the bowl. The hearts are all different colors: pale pink, yellow, lavender, green, white, and peach.

"I bet you like the pink candy hearts the best," Lucy says.

I giggle. "Well . . . everyone knows pink is my favorite color!"

Next Momma suggests a banner, but no one can think of what to put on it.

"How about 'Happy 50th Anniversary!'" Daddy suggests.

Momma shakes her head. "I think we need something more creative," she says.

My tummy grumbles, and I hold up a candy heart. It says, "Love is Sweet." I think the grown-ups need some help or Lucy and I will have to quit playing our game. Luckily, candy isn't just a yummy treat — it's also good inspiration!

"How about 'Love is Sweet!'" I shout.

"That's a great idea, Kylie Jean," Momma says. "It's perfect for the banner!"

Lucy and I each pop a pastel piece of sugary goodness into our mouths. Ugly Brother licks his right up off of the floor. It gives him a pink tongue. He looks so adorable!

We keep listening and playing our game, but pretty soon the family is fresh out of ideas. Luckily the party is still two weeks away, so the grown-ups decide to stop planning for today. That's a good thing for Lucy and me — we are almost out of candy!

Chapter 2
Be Sweet

The next day at school, our teacher, Ms. Corazón, has a note on the chalkboard. It says: "Buddy Reading today!"

We are all excited, because buddy reading is so much fun! After the announcements, we line up to go read and walk to the kindergarten classroom on the other side of the building.

When we get to the room, the teachers match us up with our reading buddies. My buddy is a little girl with blond hair.

"Hi," I say. "My name is Kylie Jean."

"My name is Summer," the little girl tells me.

Summer and I walk over to the bookshelf to pick out a book together. She holds out a book about princesses. "How about this one?"

"Perfect!" I say.

Summer and I find a spot on the story rug. I read the page, then I show her the picture.

Before long, it's time to go back to our classroom. Summer gives me a big squeezy hug. "Thank you for being my special reading buddy today!" she says.

Then she gives me some candy kisses. Yum-o!

When we get back to our classroom, Ms. Corazón has an announcement.

"I have a challenge for our class," she says. "It's called the Be Sweet project. I want everyone to try to find fourteen ways to be kind in the month of February. You'll record each kind act in your writing journal."

Everyone is so excited about the project! And we already have one thing to put in our journals. If you guessed being reading buddies, you're right! That leaves thirteen nice things to do.

I raise my hand. "Can we do more than fourteen nice things?" I ask.

Ms. Corazón smiles. "Yes, of course, Kylie Jean!"

I have so many great ideas that my brain feels more stretched out than a banana taffy twist! But before I can tell Lucy, Paula, and Cara about my plans, it's time for lunch.

I grab my lunchbox and get in line with the rest of my class. When we get to the cafeteria, everyone is talking about our project. Right away I notice that kids are being nicer to the cafeteria ladies. Everyone is saying please and thank you.

"I don't think they should be able to count please and thank you as a kindness," I say. "Those words come out as natural as breathing if you were raised up right."

"You do have a point," Lucy agrees.

"It's not up to you," Paula says. "Every student decides what to count on their own."

"I know," I tell her. "I'm just sayin' what I think."

After lunch, kids are picking up every smidge of trash off the floor and putting it in the trash can. I decide to get a rag and wipe down all the tables so the lunch ladies won't have to. That is a time-saving kindness.

While I'm busy wiping off the tables, Randall Jeremiah Johnson, a boy in my class, grabs my pink princess lunchbox and runs away. He takes off across the room shouting, "Come and get it! Come and get it!"

I decide that ignoring him is the best plan. Sooner or later, he'll give up and bring my lunchbox back. When T.J. takes something of mine to tease me, I just wait it out. Besides, I am too busy helping to deal with that silly boy!

Sure enough, Randall Jeremiah wears himself out. When all of the tables are clean, I see that he has disappeared to the playground. My lunchbox is sitting right by the door.

1. Be a kindergarten reading buddy

2. Help Miss Ruth wipe tables in the cafeteria

Chapter 3

Picking a Place

After school, Momma does not have a snack ready! At first I can't believe it, but then she tells me she has a dilemma.

"What's a dilemma?" I ask.

"It's a problem that needs to be solved," Momma explains. "I have to find someplace to have Nanny and Pa's surprise party. I was planning on using the hall at the church, but it's too small. Can you help me think of a place?"

"How about the Veteran's Hall?" I suggest. "That'd be just perfect since Pa is a veteran."

"It would be perfect," Momma agrees, "but I already called and it's booked."

As much as I want to help Momma, I can't help but think about my Be Sweet project. "We have a new project at school," I tell her. "Ms. Corazón wants us to find fourteen ways to be sweet this month. I've already been sweet two times today!"

"That's wonderful, sugar!" Momma says. "Keep up the good work."

Just then, T.J. comes in and fixes his own snack. "What are y'all talking about?" he asks.

"We're trying to figure out where to have Nanny and Pa's anniversary party," I tell him.

"My friend had a party at the Party Barn," T.J. says. "You could have it there."

"I don't know," Momma says. "I was hoping for something a little fancier."

"I think we should check it out," I say. "Nanny and Pa live on a farm, so they might like a barn!"

"You might be right," Momma says with a smile. "Thanks, T.J."

Momma calls the Party Barn and finds out the space is available, so we decide to hop in the van and go take a look at it. During the drive, we talk about more ideas for my Be Sweet project.

"You could help at out at Nanny and Pa's farm or walk Miss Clarabelle's little dog," Momma suggests.

I am still waiting for the perfect idea to hit my brain when we pull up to the Party Barn. It is so cute! It looks like a real, true barn! There are big pots of cheerful red flowers sitting out front, clean white shutters, and a door that looks just like the one at Nanny and Pa's barn!

"So far, so good," Momma says. "I sure hope the inside is as pretty as the outside!"

A lady comes outside and greets us at the door. "Hey, y'all, I'm Miss Pam. Come on in!"

Inside there are several old wood tables. Pretty red-checked curtains hug the wide windows. I can tell Momma just loves it. "This place has character!" she exclaims. "And all the red is perfect for a Valentine's Day anniversary party."

"I think it would be perfect for your party," Miss Pam says. "I'll let y'all have a look around. Let me know if you have any questions."

Momma takes pictures to show Aunt Susie. In the back of the building, there is a nice clean kitchen we can use for the party food. It even has an oven and a refrigerator.

"A person could really live here!" I say.

"Who knows?" Momma says. "Maybe Miss Pam does live here when there aren't parties."

When we're done checking everything out, we spot Miss Pam stacking some chairs.

"We should help her," I tell Momma.

Momma and I head over to help, and before long all of the chairs are put away.

"Kylie Jean, you just did another kind deed!" Momma says. "Now you only need to do eleven more sweet things. You are going to be done with this project in a snap!"

After Momma and I are finished at the Party Barn, we go next door to the Dairy Bee. Momma still owes me an afternoon snack. I decide to order the Ice Cream Dream. Yummy!

You'll never believe who's behind us in line. Randall Jeremiah Johnson is there getting ice cream, too.

I try to be sweet. "What flavor are you getting?" I ask.

"Cookie dough," he replies.

All of a sudden, Randall Jeremiah reaches up and yanks on my ponytail! My barrette with the pink bow pops off and flies across the room. It lands right on top of a little girl's ice cream. The little girl starts to cry, and Randall Jeremiah runs off.

"Oh, my!" Momma says. "We'd better get that little girl another sundae."

Once we finish our ice cream, Momma and I hurry home to start dinner before Daddy gets home from work. I save Ugly Brother a bite of my Ice Cream Dream. That dog sure does love a frosty treat!

3. Help out at the Party Barn

Chapter 4

Lonely Hearts

The next afternoon when I get on the bus home
from school, the first thing I do is offer to share my
candy with Mr. Jim. After all, candy is sweet, just
like I'm trying to be!

As we drive, I see a giant brick house with
green shutters. The yard is full of tall, strong, leafy
trees and the flowerpots are filled with all kinds
of colorful blooms. Some older folks sitting on the
porch.

I've always wondered what that house is. I decide to ask Mr. Jim. "What is that place?" I ask. "And how come there are so many people there? Are they having a party?"

"It's called Oak Manor," Mr. Jim says. "And no, they're not having a party. All those folks live there together."

"How come?" I ask.

"A lot of them are too old to live alone," Mr. Jim explains. "And some of them are sick. They need help. In fact, my momma, Miss Hattie, lives there."

"It must be real fun to live with your friends!" I say.

Mr. Jim shakes his head. "There are a lot of lonely hearts at Oak Manor," he tells me. "Some folks don't have a single soul to come and visit them. Like my momma's roommate, Miss Rose. She's all alone in the world. Miss Betty, the woman in charge there, is always looking for ways to cheer them up."

Just then an idea hits my brain like Skittles on a rainbow! As soon as I get home, I call my best cousin, Lucy.

When she answers the phone, I am so excited the words pop right out of my mouth like sugary sweet bubblegum. "I want to help the folks at Oak Manor!" I say.

"I love that idea!" Lucy says. "I want to help, too!"

Lucy and I decide to make a list of things we can do to help.

- Write letters
- Read books or newspapers out loud
- Play cards or games
- Bring a special treat
- Make a special card
- Call on the phone to say hello
- Pick a bouquet
- Deliver a box of candy

"This is a great start!" I say when we're done. "Now we have all sorts of things to add to our list of sweet deeds!"

That night before I go to bed, I tell Ugly Brother all about my idea for the class project. He loves my idea so much he covers my whole face with doggie kisses.

"Thank you for the kisses," I say. "I sure do hope Ms. Corazón likes my idea as much as you do!"

Ugly Brother agrees. "Ruff, ruff." Then he looks at my list, looks back up at me, and barks some more.

"What's the matter?" I ask. "Am I missing something?"

Ugly Brother barks two more times. Finally, I catch on. "How about this?" I say. I grab a pencil and add something to the list. When I'm done writing, I show it to him again.

> ◦ Call on the phone to say hello
>
> ◦ Pick a bouquet
>
> ◦ Deliver a box of candy
>
> ◦ Bring along a special doggie visitor

Ugly Brother goes wild, chasing his tail in a circle and barking happily. "Ruff, ruff! Ruff, ruff!"

If there's one thing you can say about my dog brother, it's that he is a really good helper. And he always wants to be included.

That gives me another idea. Maybe Miss Clarabelle's doggie, Tess, will want to visit, too! After all, nothing cheers a person up quite like puppy kisses.

"Ugly Brother, would you like Tess to come, too?" I ask.

He jumps back up on my bed, licking my ear like I'm hiding a doggie bone in there. I am sure that means yes. I remind myself to ask Miss Clarabelle for permission. I just know she'll think it's a good idea!

Before I turn out the lights and go to sleep, I add one more thing to the list of sweet deeds I've done so far:

4. Share my candy with Mr. Jim

Chapter 5
Pet Peeves and Pet Projects

The next day I am so sleepy! My brain was way too busy to go to sleep last night. I tried really hard to close my eyes, but there were so many things to think about.

Usually when Momma calls up to me that it's time to get up, I am already awake, but today she has to call me two times. It takes me forever to get dressed. I wash my face and brush my hair in slow motion.

When I get downstairs for breakfast, Momma has everything on the table. "How did you sleep, Sweet Pea?" she asks.

"I was too busy thinking," I tell her. "I forgot to sleep!"

"I have an idea that will help you wake up," Momma says. "Why don't you take Miss Clarabelle's dog for a quick walk before school?"

"Good idea!" I agree. I gobble down my breakfast and slip out the back door. It's very quiet outside. It seems like the whole town of Jacksonville is still tucked in bed under the covers.

Even though I tap extra quietly on Miss Clarabelle's door, I seem to wake everyone up! Suddenly I see three cars, the newspaper boy on his bike, and two mommas out jogging.

A moment later, Miss Clarabelle opens the door. She is wearing a housecoat with teacups on it. "What a nice surprise!" she says. "Did you come for a little visit before school?"

"Momma sent me to see if your little doggie needs a walk," I explain.

"That sure is sweet of you, Kylie Jean. I am sure she would love to take a walk," Miss Clarabelle says. "Is Ugly Brother going for a walk, too?"

"No, ma'am, he's under the kitchen table waiting for T.J. to drop some food," I explain. "It'll just be a short walk for us girls so I don't miss my bus."

Miss Clarabelle clips Tess's pretty purple leash to her collar and hands it to me. We head off down the sidewalk.

Tess is a good little dog while we walk. She doesn't try to run off or bark at birds singing their morning songs in the trees.

We are headed around the block when I notice that Mr. Jones's newspaper is lying in the road. The paperboy must have missed his front porch. Tess and I stop to help. I carry his newspaper up to the porch and ring the doorbell. *Ding-dong!*

Mr. Jones comes to the door and I hand him his paper. "Here you go, Mr. Jones," I say. "This was in the street."

Mr. Jones smiles at me. "Thank you, Kylie Jean!" he says. "That's awful nice of you."

As Tess and I turn the corner to my street, I hear a rumbly rattling sound a few streets over. Uh-oh! "Hurry, Tess!" I say. "Mr. Jim's bus is coming."

We dash up the steps to Miss Clarabelle's front porch. "Thank you for letting me walk Tess," I say. "The bus is coming. See you later!"

Momma is standing at the fence with my backpack, waving for me to hurry up. I see T.J. race out the door behind her, so I'm not the only one who's late today. T.J. and I make it to the curb just as Mr. Jim is getting ready to pull away.

I take a seat behind Mr. Jim. "Were you waiting for me?" I ask him.

Mr. Jim shakes his head. "I can't wait, or everyone would be late," he tells me. "You kids are supposed to be ready to go when I drive up."

I look up and see Mr. Jim wink at me. As soon as I see that, I know he did a sweet deed for me so I wouldn't miss the bus.

"Okay, then. Thank you anyway," I say.

By the time I get to school, I feel wide awake. That walk sure did the trick! I can't wait to tell my teacher all about Oak Manor. I find Lucy, and we go talk to Ms. Corazón about my idea.

I tell our teacher about my plan, then say, "Getting more visitors for Oak Manor is my pet project!" Momma taught me that a pet project is the one you like the best.

"I love your idea," Ms. Corazón says. "I think it could it be a project for the whole class. Some of the other students might want to visit the lonely folks, too, but first we need more information."

"I can get more!" I offer. "I'll ask my momma to take me to visit Oak Manor."

When Lucy and I get back to our desks, our friends Paula and Cara are sitting there. And there's something else sitting there, too — a fancy heart-shaped box of chocolates and a pretty pink flower right on top of my desk.

"What's that?" Lucy asks.

"I don't know," I reply. "I didn't see anyone put it there."

"Is there a note?" Paula asks.

I pick up the box and turn it over. But there's nothing to tell me who it's from. "Nope," I reply, shaking my head.

"I bet it's from a secret admirer!" Lucy says. "Can I please help you open it?"

"Can we please help you eat it?" Cara asks.

"Sure!" I say. My friends and I just love chocolate.

When Lucy opens the box, we find out my secret admirer likes candy, too. One of the chocolates has a big bite out of it!

I take a chocolate for myself before passing the box to my cousin and my friends. I take a bite — mmmm! Caramel, my favorite!

As we snack on our sweet treats, I look at the candy box again. It is super mysterious. Whoever left it didn't leave a single clue — except for the nibbled piece of candy. I look around for a kid with chocolate on his or her face, but I don't see a single one.

5. Walk Miss Clarabelle's dog

6. Deliver newspaper

Chapter 6
Spreading Sweetness

That afternoon, Momma agrees to take me to Oak Manor to talk to Miss Betty, the woman in charge, about my idea. It is a warm, sunny day, so there are lots of folks sitting on the porch in rocking chairs.

"Welcome!" one man calls out.

"Who are you here to visit?" another asks.

"I'm Mrs. Carter," Momma introduces herself. "And this is Kylie Jean. We're here to see Miss Betty."

The folks on the porch nod, smile, and wave as we go inside. Momma called Miss Betty last night to ask if we could visit, so she is waiting for us in the entryway.

"Hello, there!" Miss Betty says, shaking our hands. "It's so nice to meet you both."

Miss Betty leads us into her office. There is a big desk, large windows draped with pink, rose-covered curtains, and a wall of bookshelves. Across the room are some comfy pink chairs for company to sit in.

"Please sit down," Miss Betty says.

"Thank you," Momma replies as we both take a seat. The chairs are so big and soft. Mine practically swallows me right up!

"I just love your office!" I say, looking around. "Pink is my color. Is it yours, too?"

Miss Betty gives me a sweet smile. "I am very fond of the color pink!" she confesses. "Now tell me about your idea. Your momma said it has something to do with the folks who live here."

"My class at school is working on a Be Sweet project," I say. "We are supposed to do fourteen sweet deeds in February. And since my bus driver, Mr. Jim, said there are lots of lonely folks here, I thought it would be sweet to visit with them!"

"That's a wonderful idea!" Miss Betty says. "I'm sure our residents would love some company."

"I told my teacher about my idea, and she thought my whole class should get involved," I continue.

Miss Betty looks thrilled. "We already have some volunteers," she says, "but you can never have too much company!"

Miss Betty offers to give us a tour of Oak Manor. As we're walking around, I see my friend and neighbor, Grace. She is wearing a striped apron. It is so cute!

"Hi, Grace!" I say. "Do you work here?"

"Sort of," Grace replies. "I volunteer here as a candy striper."

"What's a candy striper?" I ask. "Can I be one, too?"

"A candy striper is a special kind of volunteer," Grace says. "You have to be sixteen."

"I guess I'll just have to wait!" I reply.

Miss Betty continues our tour and shows us the dining room. It has a beautiful piano for music programs and tables so the residents can play cards and games.

Next is the living room. It has a giant, noisy TV. Two men are watching it with the volume turned all the way up.

"They can't hear very well, so they like the volume loud!" Miss Betty shouts.

Next, Miss Betty shows us where all of the residents live. Each resident shares a room with one other person. The rooms are nice and big with room for two beds and a little sitting area. Most of the rooms are decorated with photos, paintings, books, and other little treasures to make them feel like home.

At the end of our tour, Miss Betty says, "I am so happy that you picked us for your pet project, Kylie Jean. Having so many young people around will really make our residents happy."

Miss Betty gives Momma a list of the residents. It's for me to take to school so my teacher can see how many students we'll need. Then she shakes Momma's hand and mine, too. "Thank you so much," she says.

On the way home, we pass the fire station and an idea hits my brain like chocolate on fudge. "Momma, can we please bake those nice firemen some cookies?" I ask. "It'd be a sweet thing to do."

"You are full of sweet ideas!" Momma says. "Okay, but only if you don't have too much homework and promise to help clean up after."

"You've got yourself a deal!" I say.

As soon as we get home, Momma and I mix up a big batch of chocolate-chip cookies for the firefighters. The whole house smells so yummy!

When T.J. gets home, he hangs out with us for a while. I can tell he's hoping to get a cookie. "It sure smells tasty in here," he hints.

Finally, Momma gives in. "Okay, T.J., you can have a cookie." she says. "But only if you drive Kylie Jean over to the fire station so she can drop them off. I need to cook dinner."

T.J. looks and looks, but he can't find the keys to his truck. We look everywhere. T.J. checks his pockets. Momma looks by the front door. I dig through his backpack.

Suddenly I spot them — in Ugly Brother's dog dish. Silly brothers are always playing tricks on each other!

T.J. and I drive over to the fire station and deliver the cookies. Those firefighters sure are grateful — and hungry! The cookies are almost gone before T.J. and I even leave!

After dinner, Momma helps me write a letter to my teacher. We include all the things we learned today from Miss Betty about Oak Manor, including the residents who need visitors.

When we're finished, I make two new additions to my list of sweet deeds:

7. Make cookies for the firemen

8. Find T.J.'s keys

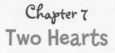

Chapter 7
Two Hearts

The next day, Momma gives me the letter we wrote for Ms. Corazón. I put it in my backpack so it'll be safe. I can't wait to give it to my teacher so we can get started on our class project right away!

On the way to school, I sit in my favorite seat, right behind Mr. Jim. "Did you go to Oak Manor yet?" he asks.

"Yup! I sure did!" I tell him proudly.

"Did you meet my momma?" Mr. Jim asks.

I shake my head. "Not yet, but maybe today I will."

When I get to my classroom, I tell Lucy, Cara, and Paula all about Oak Manor. I am so busy talking that I almost forget to give Ms. Corazón the envelope from Momma! Luckily, I remember to hand it to her right before the late bell rings.

As soon as the morning announcements are over, we start math practice. I watch as Ms. Corazón opens the letter and reads it.

Lucy leans over and whispers, "You'd better stop staring and do your math or you'll get a bad grade."

I sigh. "I know, but I'm so excited about this project and the big anniversary party that it's hard to think!" I whisper back.

At last, Ms. Corazón announces that she is
going to assign students to residents at Oak Manor
for our class project. Right
away I raise my hand
in the air. I do a little
beauty queen wave too,
just for practice . . . nice
and slow, side-to-side,
with a dazzling smile.

Ms. Corazón notices
my wave. "Yes, Kylie Jean, do you have a
question?"

"It's not really a question. It's a request," I tell
her. "Please, please, can I be assigned to Miss
Rose? She is the best friend of my bus driver's
momma."

"Okay, Kylie Jean. Since this is your pet project, you may work with Miss Rose," Ms. Corazón says. "Now who wants to be Kylie Jean's partner?"

Lucy and Randall Jeremiah Johnson raise their hands right away. They both want to help Miss Rose, too, but Lucy gets picked to be my partner. We celebrate with a quick squeezy hug.

From the corner of my eye I see Randall Jeremiah stick out his tongue at Lucy. How rude! I guess he just doesn't understand that best cousins like to do everything together.

Once all the students and residents are paired up, Miss Corazón hands out permission slips to the class.

"We'll be visiting Oak Manor after school tomorrow," she tells us. "You'll all need to get your permission slips signed if you want to go."

When I get home, I call Miss Betty right away to tell her we are coming the next day after school.

"That's wonderful, Kylie Jean!" Miss Betty says. "We can't wait to see you and your classmates tomorrow afternoon."

"I can't wait either!" I tell her.

Time is not my friend, because it will not hurry up! I have to wait all evening, all night, and all the next day at school until I can go meet Miss Rose. Finally the last bell rings, and it's time to go.

Momma is waiting for Lucy and me outside. She's going to drive us to Oak Manor. Mr. Jim will miss us, but he only stops at kids' houses, not retirement homes.

Lucy and I sit in the backseat next to the flowers Momma brought for us to give to Miss Rose. On the way, we talk about Nanny and Pa's surprise anniversary party.

"We need to get our invitations sent out soon," Momma says. "Otherwise there won't be very many guests to shout surprise!"

Lucy and I look at each other. "We'll help!" we say at the same time.

Momma smiles at us. "Okay, let's work on them together."

Miss Betty is waiting for us on the porch when we pull up. She is holding a clipboard with notes and wearing a suit the color of pink bubble gum.

"Miss Betty's color is pink, too!" I whisper to Lucy as we walk up.

"I am glad to see you girls!" Miss Betty says. "Grace is going to take you to meet Miss Rose. I have to stay here and greet the other students."

Momma hands us the flowers. Lucy and I walk over to Grace, who is waiting by the door in her candy-striper apron.

"Miss Hattie and Miss Rose live in room number two," Grace tells us as we walk down the hall. She stops outside a door. "Here we are. Two ladies in room two with two volunteers to visit them!"

Grace opens the door. "Miss Hattie, Miss Rose, you have some visitors!" she says. "Meet Kylie Jean and Lucy."

I can guess right away which one is Mr. Jim's momma. Miss Hattie is tall, just like Mr. Jim, and has gray hair. Miss Rose is tiny with white hair. I notice that their room smells good, like lemon drops and lavender.

I hand Miss Hattie a sunny bouquet of daisies, and I let Lucy give Miss Rose the bouquet of pink roses.

"Thank you,
girls," Miss Rose says,
accepting the flowers.
"That is just so sweet of
you."

"Miss Rose, would
you like us to read to
you, or do you want to
have a little chat first?"
I ask.

"How about we do both," Miss Rose replies.
"First we'll talk a bit and then you can read to
me."

I tell Miss Rose all about my family and Ugly
Brother. "Maybe I can bring him to meet you
someday," I offer.

Miss Rose tells us she used to be a librarian. On
her side of the room are three tall bookshelves full
of books. "Books are like friends," she says. "They
can keep you company."

Lucy and I go to the shelf to choose a book to read. There are so many books to choose from! Some of them look too hard for us, but then we see *The Secret Garden*.

Lucy and I sit on the floor right beside Miss Rose's chair in a pool of yellow sunshine and take turns reading. We can tell Miss Hattie is listening, too.

When it is time to go, Miss Rose gives us both big hugs. "You girls have two kind hearts," she says.

I give her a big squeezy hug back. I also have two new things to add to my list:

9. Bring flowers for new friends

10. Read to Miss Rose

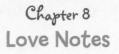

Chapter 8
Love Notes

After I get home that night, Momma and I get right to work on the invitations to Nanny and Pa's surprise party. We spread all our supplies out on the table.

We choose a pretty pink invitation. It has a shiny silver border around the edge and silver writing on it.

"What do you think?" Momma asks.

I study the
invitation. "It looks
great!" I say. "But . . .
why does it say Linda
Jo and Johnny?"

"Well, none of my
parents' friends call
them Nanny and
Pa or Momma and
Daddy," Momma
explains. "So Aunt
Susie and I decided to use their first names."

Huh. I never really thought that much about
Nanny and Pa's other names. But I guess Momma
is right. "Okay," I say after a minute. "That makes
sense."

Momma makes two piles on the table, one for cards and one for envelopes.

"What can I do to help?" I ask.

"You can put the cards in the envelopes," Momma tells me.

I take one card and put it in one envelope. Then I make a new pile of stuffed envelopes. Momma takes the envelopes and writes the addresses on them. Pretty soon Ugly Brother comes in dragging a little box.

"Ugly Brother wants to help, too!" I exclaim. "He brought a box for us to put the cards in. Right, boy?"

Ugly Brother shakes with excitement "Ruff, ruff!" he barks. That means yes!

I try to think of something else Ugly Brother can do to help. Maybe he could lick the envelopes. No, too slobbery!

Ugly Brother looks awful sad and bored. Then I remember I have to get my valentine cards ready, too, so I ask, "Do you want to help me with some special cards for the kids in my class?"

Ugly Brother perks up. "Ruff, ruff!" he barks.

I bring my cards to the table. They are so cute! All the lollipops have heart-shaped cards on them.

"Be careful," Momma says. "Ugly Brother might try to eat those."

Ugly Brother puts his paws over his face. He knows we're talking about him. I pet him on the head. "You'll be a good boy, right?" I ask.

That perks him right up. "Ruff, ruff!" he barks in agreement.

Momma gives me a pen so I can start to write names on my cards. I choose the ones that say, "For My Best Friend" for Lucy, Cara, and Paula. Then I pick out cards for the rest of my classmates.

With my valentines done, I go back to helping Momma. I start to lick the envelopes for the invitations while she finishes addressing them. Lick, lick.

Momma smiles at me while I work. "Sweet Pea, you're the sweetest girl in the world," she says. "I just hate to lick envelopes!"

"Ahh ooh," I reply. That means "I know" but my mouth is so sticky from licking envelopes that it comes out funny.

Just then T.J. brings me the phone. "It's for you."

I take the phone, but my mouth is so sticky I can't get any words out. On the other end I hear Randall Jeremiah Johnson. He says, "Kylie Jean, you remind me of a stinkbug."

Ick! I try to tell him that stinkbugs are gross, but my tongue is so sticky from licking all those envelopes I can't even say a thing.

"I love bugs!" Randall Jeremiah says. Then he just hangs up.

"Who was that?" Momma asks.

I take a big drink of water so I can answer. "Randall Jeremiah Johnson," I say. "He's in my class."

"Is that the boy who pulled your hair when we got ice cream the other day?" Momma asks.

I nod my head.

"You know, sugar, when I was in third grade, a boy named Frank liked me," Momma says. "He was always acting silly like that."

Suddenly I remember the gift on my desk the other day. I bet those chocolates were from Randall Jeremiah!

"Oh, no! Does that mean Randall Jeremiah Johnson likes me?" I ask. "What did you do about Frank?"

"Nothing," Momma tells me. "He decided he liked a girl named Jane better."

I ask, "Do you think Randall Jeremiah will find another girl and leave me alone?"

Momma smiles. "Sooner or later," she says. "But in the meantime, just treat him like a regular friend. Remember, pretty is as pretty does. You might be his first true love, so you don't want to go breaking his heart or hurting his feelings."

I sigh. It's a good thing it's time to get ready for bed, because I don't want to think about being nice to Randall Jeremiah any more today. Tomorrow I will try to be his friend, but secretly I am hoping he decides to like someone else better than me — and soon!

11. Lick envelopes for Momma

Chapter 9
Hearts, Doilies, and Happiness

The next day after school, Lucy comes over to help make some extra-special valentines for our friends at Oak Manor. We also have to make a banner for Nanny and Pa's party.

We gather up all of our art supplies and magazines and spread out all over the kitchen floor. The only problem with working on the floor is that our helper Ugly Brother gets into everything. He has a heart doily stuck on his tail and red glitter on his face!

"You are just as pretty as a picture," I tell him. "You could be Miss Rose's valentine!"

"Ruff, ruff!" Ugly Brother barks happily.

He looks so excited that I feel bad telling him I was just kidding. "Sorry, brother," I say. "But you can come visit Miss Rose anyway."

Ugly Brother seems a little sad, but I let him help me make some more cards, and he forgets all about it. I make Miss Rose's card using pictures of roses that Momma let me cut out of her gardening magazine. They look so pretty stuck on the pink heart-shaped doily.

Soon the kitchen floor is completely covered with glitter, scraps of paper, pots of paint, bottles of glue, and one-of-a-kind valentine cards waiting for their decorations to dry.

When Momma comes in, she takes a look at the mess and says, "It's a good thing you girls are doing all of your art projects at the same time. It looks to me like two projects are going to equal one super-huge mess!"

"Sorry, Momma!" I say. "We'll clean up when we're done. We promise!"

While our special cards are drying, Lucy and I get to work on a banner for Nanny and Pa's party. We roll out a long piece of white paper.

"Do you think we should put red roses on it?" Lucy suggests.

"No, they're going to have vases of them on the tables," I reply.

We are quiet while we try to think of something else. Finally Lucy says, "Do you remember where you got the idea for the words?"

"I sure do!" I reply. "Are you thinking we should use conversation hearts to decorate the banner, too?"

"Sure am!" Lucy says.

Now that we have our design decided, it's time to make the banner! First we write, "Love is Sweet" in giant red letters. Then we draw conversation hearts all around the outside. Next we add a swirly red border along the top and bottom of the banner.

When we're finished, Lucy and I clean up our gigantic mess. I wish that my best cousin could stay all night, but it's time for her to go home now. Besides, I'll be seeing lots of her since Valentine's Day is on Friday. And the next day is Nanny and Pa's surprise party!

12. Make valentines for our new friends

Chapter 10
Queen of Kindness

Today is finally Valentine's Day! Yippee!

"Happy Valentine's Day!" Momma says when I come downstairs. To celebrate, she makes heart-shaped pancakes with chocolate chips in them. They taste like a candy bar. Yum!

I give her a big squeezy hug and say, "I love you, Momma, more than bees love honey."

Just then, Daddy comes in with a little red velvet box for Momma. "Happy Valentine's Day, darlin'!" he says.

"For me?" Momma asks. She opens the box. Inside are heart-shaped diamond earrings. "Ohhh, I love them!" she says as she hugs Daddy.

Daddy kisses me on the cheek and gives me a pretty pink card. On the front it has glitter and a girl who looks like a little princess.

"Thank you, Daddy," I say. "I love you more than bears love honey."

After breakfast, I get all my things together. I have my backpack, lunchbox, cupcakes with conversation heart decorations for the class party, and a shoebox to collect my valentines.

When we get to school, everyone is so excited about the party! All my classmates brought shoeboxes to put their valentines in, too. We decorate them in the morning — I draw pink hearts all over mine.

"Your box turned out so cute!" Lucy tells me.

After lunch, we put our boxes on top of our desks so everyone can deliver their valentines. All around the room, kids are sorting out their cards and delivering them to boxes.

I see Randall Jeremiah Johnson across the room. His box is decorated with a gigantic green dinosaur eating a red heart.

Once all of our cards are passed out, the party begins. Some kids are at the party table getting treats, but Lucy, Cara, Paula, and I decide to look at our cards first.

The first valentine I grab is so big I can hardly get it out of my box. It is a card made out of notebook paper folded in half with a poem on it. It says: "Roses are red, you like pink, some dogs stink."

Roses are
red, you
like pink,
some dogs
stink

"Who gave you that?" Cara asks.

Lucy peers over my shoulder. "No one signed it," she says.

Even though it's not signed, I recognize the handwriting. It's from Randall Jeremiah Johnson. Just then I see him walking toward me with a big cupcake. Oh, no! "Let's go get our treats from the party table," I say quickly.

My friends and I head across the room. I look over just in time to see Randall Jeremiah take a humongous bite of cupcake. I guess he changed his mind about coming over to us.

When I get home from school that afternoon, I show Momma all of my cards. I save the biggest one for last. "This is the card that Randall Jeremiah Johnson gave me."

"Well, isn't that nice?" Momma says. "He even wrote you a little poem. Why don't you call him and see if he would like come to the party tomorrow?"

I'm not sure I like that idea, but Momma did say I should try to be his friend. "Okay, I guess so," I say. "But do you think I could I ask two people to come tomorrow? Randall Jeremiah and someone else?"

"Who else are you thinking of inviting?" Momma asks. "We've already invited everyone we know."

"We didn't invite Miss Rose to the party!" I say.

Momma smiles. "What a sweet idea. You go right ahead and call her."

First, I call Randall Jeremiah Johnson. "This is Kylie Jean Carter," I say when his momma answers. "May I please speak to Randall Jeremiah?"

"I'm sorry, he's not home right now," Randall Jeremiah's momma replies. "May I take a message?"

"I am his friend from school," I tell her, "and he is invited to a party tomorrow."

"I'm sure he'll want to come to the party," she says. "Thank you for inviting him."

Next I call Miss Rose. "Hi, Miss Rose!" I say when she answers. "This is Kylie Jean. I am calling to invite you to Nanny and Pa's anniversary party tomorrow. It's a surprise!"

Miss Rose says, "I would love to come to the party!"

"Did you get the special valentine I sent you?" I ask.

"I sure did! And it is just lovely!" she exclaims.

We chat for a few minutes, and before we hang up, Miss Rose says, "Thank you again for inviting me to the party, Kylie Jean. You are just the queen of kindness!"

13. Invite Miss Rose and Randall Jeremiah to the party

Chapter 11
Party Time

Cock-a-doodle-doo! The next morning we are up when the rooster crows. Today is the day of Nanny and Pa's party.

Momma, Daddy, T.J., Ugly Brother, and I all pile into the van. We are off to the Party Barn, but first we stop at the Gas and Go for donuts. This works out perfectly because Lucy and I decided to give our grandparents a special present, and I can buy it here. I will give you an itty-bitty hint: It has something to do with candy.

When we get to the Party Barn, T.J. gets a ladder from Miss Pam and starts hanging the banner Lucy and I made. "Is it straight?" he asks.

I say, "Yup!"

"It looks wonderful," Momma agrees.

A few minutes later, the florist arrives to put flowers on the tables. Some of the vases are tall and have grand-looking flowers and some are short with sweet, petite ones. The room smells heavenly with so many roses and daisies everywhere.

Just then, Daddy hollers, "Hey, y'all, I'm bringing in the cake!"

It's a huge cake decorated with lovebirds, ribbons, and gold rings. I run to hold the door open for him and bump right into Lucy. We laugh!

More helpers have arrived. Lucy and I are in charge of the candy bar. Momma brought glass jars and candy to fill them. It's like a salad bar but better because it's filled with candy instead.

"What kind of candy do we have?" Lucy asks.

I point to the different bags of candy. "We have jelly beans, chocolate kisses, lemon drops, and conversation hearts," I tell her.

"Pretty please, may I fill the conversation hearts?" Lucy asks.

I nod. "Sure! I want to do jellybeans anyway. They're my daddy's favorite."

Momma brought measuring cups for us to use as scoops. The candies sound like raindrops falling as we pour them into the jars.

Lucy finishes filling the heart candy jar and starts on the sunny lemon drops. They make a lot more noise going into the jar. It sounds like tap dancers tapping away.

The last jar gets filled with chocolate kisses. Momma got the ones in the gold wrappers since it is a golden anniversary party.

When we are all finished, we stand back to admire our work. "It's the sweetest thing I've ever seen," I say.

Lucy and I sit down to eat a few pieces of candy we saved for ourselves, but just then my big cousin Lilly walks by carrying some presents.

"Who told y'all it's break time?" Lilly says. "You'd better go see what they want you to do next. We've got a party to get ready for."

Lilly is right! Lucy and I spend the next hour blowing up balloons and setting out food trays, plates, and napkins. Finally everything is ready except for us!

My whole family jumps into the van and dashes home to change for the party. Momma and I put on our matching dresses with pink flowers on them. I tie a pink bow around Ugly Brother's neck so he can look fancy for the party, too.

Soon we are back at the Party Barn. We have to greet all the guests as they arrive.

Randall Jeremiah Johnson's momma drops him off. He follows Lucy and me everywhere. I see Miss Rose there, too, visiting with Granny and Pappy.

Right before one o'clock, we all get quiet as mice. Then Nanny and Pa walk in.

"SURPRISE!" everyone shouts.

Nanny and Pa smile and laugh. Nanny is so happy she even cries a little! I see Momma hug her and hand her a hanky.

"How did you keep this a secret?" Pa asks.

"It wasn't easy, but we wanted it to be special," Momma tells him. "You two deserve it!"

14. Fill candy jars and set the tables

15. Throw a surprise party!

Chapter 12
Secrets

When it's time to cut the cake, Lilly, Lucy, and I get to be servers and pass out cake to the guests. It's fun at first, but I get tired of asking people if they want chocolate or vanilla cake.

When everyone has cake, Pa stands up to make a speech. "Fifty years is a long time to be hitched to one gal," he starts.

Everyone laughs, and Pa continues. "But I am still married to the prettiest girl in town! She's my best friend and my wife."

"If we get mad at each other, we never stay mad," Nanny adds. "And we laugh together all the time. We like each other and love each other a lot! We want to thank y'all for this fabulous surprise party."

"Nanny, tell us the story of how you met," Lucy and I beg.

"Okay," Nanny agrees. "I remember it like it was yesterday. Your pa was a football star, and I was the new girl in town. I didn't know a single soul, and that made me feel nervous."

Nanny smiles at Pa. "On my first day, I got mixed up and went to the wrong classroom. Your pa was in his science class when I walked in wearing my pink poodle skirt. It was love at first sight."

Pa leans over and kisses Nanny sweetly on her cheek. Then she continues, "When the teacher realized I was in the wrong place, your pa offered to walk me to my English class. When we got to the door, I looked into his big brown and eyes, and I fell in love, too."

When she finishes her story, Nanny has tears in her eyes again. But this time she's not alone — Momma and Aunt Susie are crying happy tears, too.

Pa gives Nanny another sweet kiss. Then he says, "Let's open some presents!"

Nanny and Pa have lots of gifts to open. They get gold picture frames, plates that say "Happy 50th Anniversary" in gold letters, and cards full of well wishes.

Lucy and I are getting nervous. Nanny and Pa are getting some really nice gifts. I sure hope they like ours.

Finally we can't wait anymore, so we take Nanny and Pa the special gift we got them. It is wrapped in a pretty little box with two bows on top. I picked  the pink bow, and Lucy picked a white one.

"Can you open our present next?" I ask.

Lucy hands it to Pa, but he hands it over to Nanny. "Why don't you open this one, darlin'?" he says. "It looks extra special."

Nanny takes her time opening our gift, being careful not to rip the pretty paper. Finally she opens the lid and looks inside. Pa leans over to see, too. They both smile. Inside are two giant diamond candy rings.

Pa laughs and asks, "Are you going to wear yours or eat it?"

"I might just do both!" Nanny says.

Pa slips Nanny's ring on her finger. "Does this remind you of our wedding day?" he asks.

Nanny smiles at him. "This is even better," she says. "Our girls and our grandchildren are with us now!"

This is the best Valentine's Anniversary Day ever!

Then Randall Jeremiah Johnson gives me a little box.

"It's not my party," I tell him.

"I know," he says. "But I got you something anyway."

I open the box. Inside is a candy necklace with a note that says:

For: Kylie Jean
my Valentine Queen
From: Jeremiah

I put on the necklace, remembering what Momma said about breaking hearts. "Thank you!" I say. "I am happy to be the Queen of Valentine's Day and your friend."

Randall Jeremiah smiles. "Okay," he says. Then he adds, "Can I have a bite of your necklace?"

Boys are so silly! Randall Jeremiah, Lucy, Ugly Brother, and I decide to go sit by the candy bar, because we'd rather eat candy than cake.

I look around the Party Barn at all my family and friends and smile sweetly as I eat my candy. I sure do feel like a real, true Valentine Queen!

16. Celebrate Nanny and Pa's surprise party!

Marci Bales Peschke was born in Indiana, grew up in Florida, and now lives in Texas with her husband, two children, and a feisty black-and-white cat named Phoebe. She loves reading and watching movies.

When **Tuesday Mourning** was a little girl, she knew she wanted to be an artist when she grew up. Now, she is an illustrator who lives in South Pasadena, California. She especially loves illustrating books for kids and teenagers. When she isn't illustrating, Tuesday loves spending time with her husband, who is an actor, and their two sons.

Glossary

anniversary (an-uh-VUR-suh-ree)—a date that people remember because something important happened on that date in the past

challenge (CHAL-uhnj)—something difficult that requires extra work or effort to do

conversation (kon-vur-SAY-shuhn)—when you talk with someone for a while

decorate (DEK-uh-rate)—adding things to make something prettier

mysterious (miss-TIHR-ee-uhss)—very hard to explain or understand

permission (pur-MISH-uhn)—if you give permission for something, you say that you will allow it to happen

project (PROJ-ekt)—a plan or proposal

request (ri-KWEST)—something that you ask for

resident (REZ-uh-duhnt)—someone who lives in a particular place

veteran (VET-ur-uhn)—someone who has served in the armed forces, especially during a war

Talk!

1. Talk about your favorite holiday. Is it Valentine's Day or a different holiday? What do you like about that holiday?

2. Kylie Jean didn't know what to do when Randall Jeremiah was teasing her. What are some other things she could have done?

3. What do you think happens after this story ends? Talk about what else might happen at Nanny and Pa's surprise party.

Be Creative!

1. Pretend that it's Valentine's Day. Create a special valentine for someone you know.

2. Do your own Be Sweet project! Make a list of sweet deeds you do during the next week.

3. Pretend that you are in charge of planning a surprise party. Who would you invite? What would your theme be? What decorations would you choose?

This is the perfect treat for any Valentine Queen!
Just make sure to ask a grown-up for help.

Love, Kylie Jean

SWEETHEART COOKIES

YOU NEED:

1 tube of premade cookie dough, sugar-cookie flavor

Pink frosting

Red, white, and pink sprinkles

A heart-shaped cookie cutter

A rolling pin

A cookie sheet

A grown-up helper

1. Ask your grown-up to help you roll out the cookie dough into a 1/2-inch thick circle. Use your cookie cutter to cut out heart shapes.

2. Bake the cookies as directed, with grown-up help, watching to make sure they don't get too crispy. Cool completely.

3. Decorate each cookie with pink frosting. Add sprinkles to the top to make your sweet treats sparkle!

Yum, yum!

THE FUN DOESN'T STOP HERE!

Discover more at www.capstonekids.com

💜 Videos & Contests
❀ Games & Puzzles
💜 Friends & Favorites
❀ Authors & Illustrators

Find cool websites and more books like this one at www.facthound.com. Just type in the Book ID: **9781479523528** and you're ready to go!